C016495392

The
Snow
Cat

www.hollywebbanimalstories.com

STRIPES PUBLISHING
An imprint of Little Tiger Press
1 The Coda Centre, 189 Munster Road,
London SW6 6AW

This hardback edition first published
in Great Britain in 2016.

ISBN: 978-1-84715-663-1

The
Snow
Cat

HOLLY WEBB

Stripes

For Charlotte Fennell

~ HOLLY WEBB

To Sandy and Diana – cat rescuers

~ JO

CHAPTER ONE

"Do you like it, Bel?" Gran smiled at her.

"I don't know. I think so – but it's so different." Bel looked around the little living room of the flat. It was such an odd mixture – all Gran's old things, but in new places, and looking a bit squashed and awkward.

"I know it feels strange, dear, but it'll be so much easier for me living here than it was in my old house. Hardly any cleaning to do, and no stairs. And it'll be nice having neighbours so close. You'll still see me, Bel love, don't worry."

Bel nodded uncertainly. She already knew all that. Mum and Gran had explained it to her. And she'd seen that Gran was getting frailer, and finding it hard to get up and down the stairs. But it still felt weird, knowing that she wouldn't be living in the house down at the end of the road any more. Bel couldn't pop in and see her after school, not in the same way. Oak House, the sheltered housing Gran had moved to, was a few minutes' drive away. It wasn't the same at all.

"It's such a lovely old house," Mum said. "I wonder who lived here before? It feels as though a house like this should have so many stories."

Gran nodded. "They gave me a little booklet about the history of the house. I've put it down somewhere, I can't quite remember where. But I'll show it to you both when I find it. The house was built in the 1850s, I remember that much. And the gardens were laid out then, too. They're quite old-fashioned, with the shrubbery and the fish ponds, but I love them. They'll be so nice for sitting in on sunny days."

Bel wasn't quite sure what a shrubbery was, but she loved the gardens, too. They were huge, and even just coming up the drive she'd seen a couple of statues, and a glint of water from a lily pond. It was almost like Gran was living in a stately home.

"Why don't you go and explore?" Gran suggested.

"Am I allowed?"

"Of course you are! If anyone asks why you're there, just explain that you're visiting me," Gran said, and Mum nodded encouragingly.

"It'll be fine."

Bel looked out of the window – it was a sunny autumn afternoon, and there were drifts of leaves under the great trees. She felt like running across the grass, and kicking the leaves up in clouds, but the gardens looked so empty, and lonely. "All right," she murmured, a little reluctantly.

"You can go straight out here, look." Gran pointed to some tall glass doors.

"I'm lucky to have a flat on the ground floor – it's lovely just to be able to walk out into the gardens. And I can sit here by the doors and watch the squirrels."

Bel smiled. She could see a squirrel now, chasing along one of the low branches of a big horse chestnut tree. Maybe it was where he had his nest. Suddenly she felt a lot more cheerful. She let herself out on to the narrow paved terrace outside the glass doors, and then hurried down the steps, planning to see how close she could get to him. She loved squirrels – they had such neat little ears, and sparkling black eyes, and they always looked clever. Mum said they dug up the tulip bulbs in her flowerpots when they came into the garden at home, but Bel thought it was worth it.

Bel set off across the lawn, walking

slowly so as not to scare the squirrel away. She was glad she had her thick cardigan on – it was one that Gran had knitted for her, white and made like a sort of fluffy jacket. She was only wearing it because they were visiting Gran, it was a bit old-fashioned and babyish-looking, but Bel knew it would make Gran happy to see her in it. Still, she shivered a little as she crossed the grass. It was only late October, but the weather was already getting really chilly. There had been a frost that morning – she could still see patches of it on the shaded parts of the grass, where the sun hadn't melted it away.

Bel sighed as the squirrel spotted her coming, and dashed up to the top of his tree, chattering crossly. Perhaps he wasn't used to there being many visitors.

Or maybe he thought she was after his winter stores. She waved to him and walked on, making for the dark clumps of trees beyond the lawn. Maybe this was what Gran had called the shrubbery? It looked to Bel like a small wood, full of fir trees and evergreen bushes. They were set out in clumps, with little paths winding in-between them, Bel realized as she got closer. And there were statues, too, here and there among the trees. As though this was a place made for walking around and admiring. The tall glossy-leaved bushes cut out the cold wind as she slipped into the grove. It was a good place to play on a chilly day.

Bel walked all round, looking at the statues – there were so many. Her favourite was a little boy, just at the entrance to the shrubbery. At first she thought he was wearing furry trousers, but then she saw he had hooves, too – he was half-goat. She found another fish pond, a tiny one, full of darting golden-orange fishes. She crouched beside the pond, watching them for a while, and then heard her mum calling across the lawn.

"You were gone for ages," Gran said, smiling. "Did you find some nice places to explore?"

"I was in the shrubbery – those trees over there. That is the shrubbery, isn't it?" Bel pointed. "There's a pond, with fish in it. The gardens are amazing, Gran."

"So you like my new home, then?" Gran smiled at her. "You can come and stay, you know. I made sure that I got one of the flats with a spare room. It's fairly snug, but there's just enough space for you and a bed, Bel. It would be lovely if you could come and see me and have sleepovers, like you used to in the old house."

Bel hugged her. "Of course I will."

CHAPTER TWO

The weather got colder and colder as the months went by, and Bel and her mum and dad visited Gran at Oak House every few days. Gran had caught a bad cough which had left her feeling really tired, but she liked to have visitors to cheer her up. She said it was much too chilly for her to go out. Bel didn't mind. She liked seeing Gran, and Gran always let her go out to look at the gardens, too. Bel had explored all the bits that were close to the house by now. There were woods further away, where the gardens joined on to the town, but she hadn't bothered with those. The trees were all overgrown and muddy, and they didn't look that exciting.

Sometimes Mum dropped Bel off at Oak House to chat to Gran while she did the shopping, and they'd sit together on Gran's little sofa and look at photos. Gran had so many albums and she loved looking through them with Bel, telling her the stories behind all the pictures. There were only a few photos of Gran herself when she was a little girl, growing up in the 1940s, but there were lots of Bel's mum, and her uncle Pete. Gran always said that Bel looked exactly like Mum did when she was a child, and Bel could see it a little bit.

There were loads of photos of all Gran's different pets as well. She loved animals, and Mum and Uncle Pete had had a dog when they were growing up, and two cats, and a rabbit. Bel was really jealous. Gran had owned eleven different cats over the years, and Bel knew all their names from their pictures. Her favourite was Tiggy, who was a pretty ginger cat with a perfect white shirt front, but Gran said she'd loved them all. Gran's last cat, Sally, who was black with golden-yellow eyes, had died a year ago, and Gran hadn't got another kitten. Bel had hoped she would, but now she understood that Gran had known she was going to move somewhere like Oak House, where pets weren't allowed.

Bel bounded into Gran's flat one afternoon just before the Christmas holidays, so excited that she could hardly get the words out. "Guess what! Guess!"

"I don't know!" Gran said, laughing.

"Mum and Dad said we might be able to get a cat of our own soon!"

Gran beamed at her. "No! Oh, that's such good news, Bel. You'll love that."

"You can come and visit it," Bel

suggested. Then she grinned. "Or maybe I could sneak it in to see you! I bet I could hide a kitten in a rucksack – no one would see!"

It was such a shame, Bel thought later that afternoon, as she was flicking through the pictures in Gran's album. Sally would have loved exploring the gardens, and she was sure a new kitten would, too. But maybe if all the residents had cats or dogs or rabbits there would be fights. She supposed it did make sense really.

Bel looked down at the photo of Sally, stretched out in a patch of sun in Gran's old garden. "Do you miss her, Gran?"

Gran sighed. "Of course I do. And I miss having a cat now that I'm here.

But there are plenty of other nice things about this house, Bel. I went to a dance class yesterday, did I tell you that? Salsa! They have all these clubs and classes in the old drawing room on the ground floor."

Bel giggled at the thought of Gran and the other elderly residents she'd met doing dramatic salsa dancing.

"Don't smirk," Gran scolded her, laughing. "It was a lot of fun. And some of us are very good dancers, even if we do have to take it slowly."

Bel hugged her. Actually, Gran was a great dancer and she'd helped Bel with her ballet routines in the past.

"By the way, Bel," said Gran. I found the booklet with all the information about this house when I was tidying up yesterday. There's a picture in it that I think you'll like. You get it, look, it's over there on the table. Now I'm sitting down it'll take me ages to get up!"

Bel fetched the booklet, and Gran flicked through the pages until she found a photo of a sad-faced girl in an old-fashioned and very frilly sort of dress, holding a big white cat in her arms. "Isn't he gorgeous?" Bel said, admiringly.

Gran laughed at her. "Yes, and the little girl's very pretty, too. Trust you to only look at the cat, Bel. But she's got a nice face, don't you think? Although she does look rather sad. Then that could just be because photographs took such a long time in the olden days. You had to stand still for ages." Gran peered at the caption. "This is one of the girls who used to live in the house."

"When's this picture from?" Bel asked, frowning. "How old would she be now?"

"Mmm. Well, she looks about your age, and this is from 1860, so let's say she was born in 1851."

Bel stared at Gran in surprise – that was ages ago. She frowned to herself, working it out. "That's more than a hundred and sixty years! But then, she must have died years ago…" She shivered. The girl was gazing out at her, cuddling her cat. She looked like she could be one of Bel's friends from school, dressed up for a school play. It was strange – almost scary – to think how long ago this picture had been taken.

"Can I read the rest of the booklet?" she asked. She was wondering if there might be more about the family. Maybe even another picture of the girl with the cat.

"Of course you can. I'll go and make some tea, and find a snack for you." Gran levered herself out of her armchair, leaving Bel to read.

The booklet was all about Oak House

before it had become sheltered housing. The house had been built in the late 1850s, it explained, so the girl's family must have been the first people to live there. Bel pursed her lips in a surprised little whistle. The house had probably been built for them. Imagine being rich enough to have an enormous house like this, built just for you. She wondered if the girl in the picture was really spoilt. Or maybe not – she'd learned about Victorian children at school. They'd gone on a visit to a museum, and there had been a Victorian schoolroom, with desks and slates to write on, and all the girls had dressed up in frilly pinafores. Mrs Abbott had explained that Victorian children were meant to be seen and not heard, and that rich children would be looked after by servants most of the time and might hardly see their parents at all. It sounded so sad. But not everyone could have been like that, Bel decided. The girl did look a bit serious, but not actually miserable.

She skimmed through the rest of the booklet – the family had been called the Armstrongs, and they owned a biscuit factory, not far away from where Bel lived. There was a picture of a beautiful tin of Armstrong's Biscuits, too, with a little girl playing in the snow on the front.

The last few pages were about the gardens, and the famous designer who had helped to set them out. There was a paragraph about the little patch of woodland that Bel had seen, too. There was an oak tree that had been growing there for hundreds of years, it said.

The house had been named after it. She frowned, trying to remember an enormous oak tree. Perhaps it was further in, or the woods were more overgrown now.

"Isn't it interesting?" Gran said, as she came back with tea and some squash and biscuits for Bel. "I remember Armstrong's Biscuits, you know. They shut the factory down when I was a little girl. They have some of those pretty tins in a case in the main entrance hall now, you could have a look." The doorbell rang. "Oh, that must be your mum. Her shopping hasn't taken long, then."

Bel put down the booklet – she'd finish reading it another day – and went to open the door. Gran made another cup of tea for Mum, then Mum and Gran started chatting about one of the neighbours.

It wasn't very interesting, so Bel went to look out of the window. She was hoping to spot that funny squirrel again, but she couldn't see him anywhere. Maybe he was asleep in his nest. Her wildlife magazine said squirrels didn't really hibernate, they just slept a lot when it got colder, and it was definitely cold enough. It was halfway through December now, and the puddles were all frozen over in the mornings when they walked to school. If she was a squirrel, she'd definitely want to be tucked up asleep in a little hole somewhere.

Something moving caught her eye, and she pressed her nose against the glass, peering at the bushes. Was that him? But it had looked white... Bel smiled excitedly. Maybe it was a white squirrel! A special winter one!

But then a white cat stepped out from the bushes. Even though he was quite far away across the lawn, Bel was sure he could see her. He gazed at her seriously for a moment, before padding slowly away, back into the trees.

"There was a cat!" she burst out, turning back to look at Gran. "A beautiful white one, just like in that photo! I thought no one here had any pets."

Gran smiled at her. "No one does, Bel. We're not allowed, you know that. Perhaps it was that funny little squirrel. I've seen him lots."

"No, it was definitely a cat," Bel insisted. "I saw him, as clear as anything."

"Maybe he came from one of the houses on the other side of the wall," Mum suggested. "It's not really that high, is it? I'm sure a cat could climb it."

"Or perhaps it's a ghost cat," Gran said, smiling.

Bel frowned. She didn't like the idea. Somehow, having read all about the Armstrong family, and the way Oak House used to be, it felt different being here now. There was a history to the house. She could almost see it, the way it was before it was divided up into lots of little flats. That girl in her frilly dress was ghosting through the hallway and up and down the stairs…

Bel was silent as she and Mum put on their coats, and got ready to leave. Then Gran hugged her goodbye, and said, "I've just realized, Bel! The next time you come, it'll be to stay! It's so exciting. And you'll be having a lovely trip, Susie." She hugged Mum, too. "I'm jealous of you, seeing those Christmas markets. Maybe you can buy me some nice little Christmas decorations for my flat."

Bel didn't say anything to Gran. She got into the car next to Mum, staring out of the window, and worrying.

"Sweetheart, is there something the matter?" Mum asked, as they hung their coats up back at home. "You've hardly said anything since we left Gran's."

Bel swallowed. "Mum, I'm not sure I want to go and stay."

"Why not? You love staying with Gran!" Mum stared at her.

"I know… But Oak House is different from Gran's real house. It's so old… There – there might be things…"

"Oh, Bel!" Mum reached over and gave her a hug. "Is it because Gran said there might be a ghost cat? I know you don't like ghost stories. But they're not true. And just because a house is old, it doesn't make it scary. Think about all the lovely things that have happened in that house! All the Christmases and birthday parties!"

"I suppose so," Bel whispered. "And Gran would be sad if I didn't go."

Mum grinned at her. "So would Dad and I, sweetie. And remember, we're going to find some lovely things for you while we're away. I'd better add some nice Christmas decorations for your gran to my list, too..." She whipped a little notebook out of her handbag, and scribbled it down.

Bel sighed. They didn't have any Christmas decorations up yet. And if she was going off to Gran's on the first weekend of the holidays, she wouldn't be able to go Christmas shopping with her friends, either. Of course she wanted Mum and Dad to go on their special trip. It was just... Them being away made everything feel different. The Christmas holidays had started, but they hadn't even bought their tree yet. Mum had said they'd do it as soon as she and Dad got back, but without a Christmas tree, and all the other lovely things they usually did, Bel just didn't feel properly Christmassy.

CHAPTER
THREE

"You're so clever, Gran!" Bel said admiringly, looking down at the biscuits she'd just helped lift out of the oven.

"I thought you'd like them," her gran said, laughing. "You didn't believe it would work, did you?"

Bel smiled and shook her head. When Gran had said they were going to make stained-glass biscuits, she'd decided there was no way they'd look anything like the beautiful ones in the recipe book. But there they were – star-shaped biscuits, with glowing red and green and yellow stars in the middle, made out of melted sweets.

"Mind you, we haven't got them off the tray yet," Gran pointed out. "Better let them cool down for a bit before we try. Why don't we decorate my little tree?

Then we can thread some of the biscuits with ribbons and hang them on, too – of course, if any stick to the tray, we'll just have to eat them, won't we?"

"They're lovely. Thanks, Gran." Bel hugged her. "It feels more like Christmas, now we're going to put up some decorations."

"Yes, well, I've got all those lovely clay ornaments that your mum and your uncle Pete made when they were at school, and those beautiful glittery snowflakes you made me. And I know my tree's only tiny, Bel, but I've been looking forward to decorating it with you. I even splashed out on some new tinsel after what your dad said about mine last year."

Bel giggled. "It *was* looking a bit shabby, Gran."

"I expect that tinsel was older than you, Bel. Possibly even older than your dad. Have a look in that bag over there, I had a lovely time shopping for some new bits."

"There's loads!" Bel pulled out fat strings of glittering gold and silver tinsel. "You could cover the whole tree!"

"I thought we could put some up round the windows as well, and along the mantelpiece." Gran sighed. "It's a little plain in here, don't you think, Bel? Some Christmas decorations will cheer it up."

Bel nodded, looking around at the room. It *was* plain – all the paint was very white, and quite boring. It wasn't at all like Gran's old house. Suddenly Bel felt a bit selfish. She'd got herself so worried about staying here with Gran, but if it was strange for her, just staying the weekend, how weird was it for Gran, living here all the time?

"I think it's nice," she said firmly. "You get to do everything new, like the new tinsel. It's going to be beautiful, Gran, I promise."

"Will you be all right, Bel?" Gran asked that night, looking down at her a little worriedly. "You're not missing your mum and dad too much?"

"No." Bel smiled at her. "Their plane must be taking off about now. It's nice they get to have a special holiday. And we're having fun, too. I loved making the biscuits, and putting the decorations up."

It was almost true. She wasn't really missing her parents, but she was still just a tiny bit worried about being in this strange house. When Mum had dropped her off that afternoon, Bel hadn't been able to stop looking over her shoulder as they walked through the entrance hall and along the corridor. She kept almost-seeing things. Movements, always just behind her, as though there was someone following her, but darting out of sight every time she turned. The huge velvet curtains further down the hall seemed to billow a little, as though someone was hiding behind them, and there was the faintest breath of laughter in the air.

It wasn't scary, exactly. It was just *weird*. And now that Gran was turning off the light and leaving her, her heart started to beat faster. Bel wasn't going to make a fuss – Gran wanted their weekend together to be so special. Still, her fingers were tightly gripped around the edge of the duvet and she even considered pulling it over her head…

But nothing happened. She could hear Gran, softly humming to herself as she pottered around in the living room. There was a gentle line of light down the side of her door – she had asked Gran to leave it open a bit. It made the darkness of her room look only grey, and soft. She could pick out the darker shapes of the furniture, and her bag, sitting on top of the chest of drawers. There were no strange flickering movements, no odd noises. She'd been imagining it. Gran was humming Christmas carols, and every so often she broke out into singing, when she could remember the words. It was nice. Comforting. Bel's eyelids closed, then wobbled, then closed again, and she wriggled herself into a ball.

When she woke up, something was different. Bel couldn't work out what it was. It couldn't be the middle of the night, because her room was quite light, even though the window was only tiny.

But everything was so quiet and still.

Bel climbed out of bed, thinking she'd go and see Gran. She'd forgotten to bring her watch, and she wasn't sure if it was time to get up. If Gran was still asleep, she'd just creep back into her room and read.

She pulled on the cardigan that Gran had knitted for her over her nightie, and tiptoed out into the living room. But then suddenly she stopped, and hopped up and down with excitement. It had snowed! She ran to the glass doors to look. The snow was banked up against the glass almost to her knees, and outside the gardens were completely white. The snow was thick, too. Everything was blurred and strange under the snowy blanket, so that as Bel pressed her nose against the glass, she could hardly tell what was where. Was that the funny little statue of the boy with goat's legs? And the steps that led down to the pond with the little golden fish had practically disappeared.

Bel whirled round, eager to go and tell Gran, but when she peeked round her door, she saw Gran was still asleep. Bel sighed. Mum had told her very seriously to remember that Gran was an old lady. No waking her up really early in the morning, Mum had been firm about that.

Bel nibbled her bottom lip. Surely Gran would *want* to be woken up to know that it had snowed? Bel would be furious if *she* was asleep and no one told *her*... But then, it was so very, very quiet. Maybe it was too early. And Gran still looked fast asleep. Bel sighed, and then brightened a little. Just because Gran was asleep, it didn't mean *she* had to stay inside, did it? She ran to fetch her wellies, and wound her big scarf round her neck. Then she unlocked the glass doors, and crept outside.

The snow had brought a great stillness. Bel turned slowly on the terrace, listening to it. It felt magical – as though she was the only person in the world out in the snow. It was a great secret that only she knew.

Bel couldn't even hear any cars going along the road. "Mum wouldn't like driving in this weather," she whispered to herself. "Maybe lots of people are staying at home."

The smooth whiteness of the gardens called to her, and with a squeak of excitement she dashed out on to the snow-covered grass, stumbling through the thick snow and giggling to herself. The crisp snow squeaked and crunched under her feet. Then she stopped, looking back at her line of prints, all the way across the perfect white lawn.

She really was alone. Bel's smile faded a little. It had been so magical, thinking that she was only person who knew about the snow, but now that single line of footprints made her feel lonely. If she'd been at home she'd have been straight on the phone to her friends Lizzie and Kate, suggesting they met up to go sledging. They wouldn't have minded being woken up, she was sure. But all on her own it just wasn't the same. And she was cold. She should have put her coat on, but she'd been so eager to get outside.

Bel sighed. Perhaps she'd go back and see if Gran was awake. Even if she couldn't come out and play in the snow, Gran could stand by the windows and watch while Bel made snow angels, and maybe a snowman. Or a snow cat! And perhaps she'd make

Bel hot chocolate, and they could drink it together. It would be a little bit like having someone to play with.

Bel was just turning to head back to the house when a movement in the shrubbery caught her eye. The squirrel? Or could it be that white cat again? Bel's heart beat a little faster, as she thought of ghost cats, but she didn't run back to the house. She peered in between the tall bushes, trying to see him again, but all was still at last. Then she gasped. There it was – just the faintest twitch of movement.

Then whatever it was moved again, and at last Bel saw. The cat. The huge white cat, with clear gold-green eyes. Even though it was so big, the snow still came halfway up its legs, and it looked miserable. If it had walked across the lawn, Bel thought, the snow would be practically up to its chest, but the snow in the shrubbery wasn't so deep – the trees and bushes had sheltered the ground a little. As Bel watched, the white cat shook out one paw distastefully, laying back its ears. Clearly it did not want to be out in this wet white stuff. Bel held back a laugh, not wanting to scare it away.

"Where did you come from?" Bel whispered. "I saw you once before! I knew I'd seen you. Gran almost had me convinced that you were a ghost, as no one here has any pets." She crouched down, ignoring the way her nightie trailed in the snow. "You're not a ghost, are you? No, you're lovely! You're such a beautiful puss. Come on. Come and see me."

The cat eyed her for a moment, then

it stalked towards her, still graceful even in the thick snow. It sat down in front of Bel, staring at her. Bel made purring noises, and murmured nonsense about how beautiful it was, until the cat leaned forward to nudge its head against her knees, and began to purr. It had the deepest purr that Bel had ever heard, a great low rumble that she could feel as well as hear. "Oh, you're gorgeous," she said. The cat purred even louder, and nuzzled at her as she rubbed its soft white ears.

Bel fussed over it for a while, but then the cat stood up, gazing up at her with gold-green eyes. It licked her hand with one little dab of its pink tongue, and then turned around and began to walk away, further into the shrubbery.

Bel sighed as she watched. She wished she could play with the cat for a little longer, but perhaps it was going home for breakfast. She should go back, too – it was so cold, and Gran was sure to be awake soon.

Then the cat stopped and stared at her. It even walked a step or two back towards her, and then let out an inviting little mew.

"Do you want me to follow you?" Bel asked hopefully. It wasn't that cold, not really. And Gran would be able to see where she'd gone – her footprints were there, as clear as anything. She followed the cat between the dark laurel bushes, smiling. The white cat liked her! Bel couldn't wait to have a cat of her own. Mum had mentioned that most kittens were born in the summer, so they might have to wait a while, but she and Bel had already started checking the website for the local shelter, just in case some kittens were brought in.

Now this strange cat wanted her to play – surely that meant she'd be good at looking after her own kitten when she got one at last?

She pushed her way gently between the snowy laurel branches, and came out on to the path that led to the little fish pond. The white cat ran in front of her, its tail waving, and Bel followed, laughing at the way it picked up its cold paws. The cat kept going, turning back every so often to see that Bel was following. Then at last it stopped by a large fir tree with low, spreading branches that swept almost to the ground. It was beautiful – Bel had noticed it before, she'd even said to Gran that it would look amazing with fairy lights draped around it. The cat looked at Bel again, and then vanished under the tree.

"Oh!" Bel crouched down to see where it had gone, just in time to see the tip of its white tail disappearing further under the branches. It was quite dry underneath, and instead of snow there was a honey-coloured carpet of sweet-smelling pine needles. It wasn't as dark as Bel had expected, either – there was much more space under the tree than she'd imagined. Stooping, Bel followed the cat, crawling over the sweetly scented needles. It seemed to take a long time, for such a short distance, and the branches were catching on the back of her cardigan, or something was. She had to claw and pull her way through the very last part, and she hoped she hadn't torn the collar. But at last she could see out on to the sparkling snow.

"I found you!" Bel panted, as she caught up with the cat, just at the very tips of the pine branches. The white cat purred thunderously at her, and put its fat white paws on her knees to reach up and lick her chin with its raspy pink tongue. Bel put her arms around it, picking it up to hug it as she came out from under the tree at last.

She turned round to look up at the tree – it had felt so much larger when she was crawling underneath it, and now it wasn't so very tall, after all. Then the white cat wriggled in her arms, and mewed a little, staring back over Bel's shoulder. Bel turned round slowly.

Standing on the path in the snow, just in front of her, was another girl. She was dressed in a full-skirted dark red coat, with a deep velvet collar and cuffs. There was a feathered hat in her hands, and her fair curly hair was rather messy, as though she'd just pulled the hat off.

The white cat sprang out of Bel's arms, and ran to rub itself around the stranger's shiny black buttoned boots, and the two girls stared silently at each other.

CHAPTER FOUR

"Have you come from the village?" the strange girl asked, but Bel could only stare at her. There were no other children at Oak House, everyone had said so. Mrs Greening, who had the flat next door to Gran, had told Bel it was so nice to see her, that children in the house made it feel more Christmassy.

"Of course you have." The girl smiled at her. "It doesn't matter. *I* don't mind. My papa might, I mean, you're not really allowed to be here, but I'm glad you are. It's nice to have someone to play with – snow isn't the same when you're on your own. How did you climb over the wall? You must be a very good climber." She peered down at Bel's wellies. "I expect those odd-looking boots help."

Bel swallowed, trying to summon up a voice, and something to say. "They're waterproof," she muttered huskily at last.

"Oh, well, that's very good for being in the snow." The girl nodded wisely. Then she looked over her shoulder in a furtive sort of way. "I ought to be wearing galoshes, but I couldn't find where my governess had put them."

"You have a governess?" Bel asked. It sounded so grand.

"Of course I do! Well, I'd rather go to school, but Papa doesn't want us to live away from home, so we have a governess instead. Don't you…?" Her voice trailed off a little, and her pale cheeks flushed pink. "I'm sorry, no, you wouldn't be able to afford a governess. I suppose you go to the village school, don't you?"

"I – I go to the school close to my house," Bel said slowly. This conversation seemed very confusing. The white cat was still twining itself around the girl's ankles, purring and purring, as though it knew her. "I'm visiting my gran," she explained. "I didn't know there were any other children here. Who did you come to see?"

"No one!" The girl laughed. "I *live* here. This is my house. I'm Charlotte Armstrong." She waved at the huge building behind them. Bel glanced at it, and then frowned, staring harder. Oak House looked different, somehow...

"My name is Isabella. But everyone calls me Bel," she murmured, taking a few steps through the trees to look more closely at the house.

The front steps were different, she realized. There was no wheelchair ramp, and there was one huge wooden door, painted dark green, instead of the glass double doors that she'd gone through so many times to see Gran. And through one of the windows she could see an enormous Christmas tree – not a silver tinsel one, like the one Gran had shown her in the main lounge, but a dark fir tree, glittering with soft golden candlelight. Real candles, Bel was almost sure.

Bel turned back and looked again at the girl. At Charlotte. At her polished black buttoned boots, her smart red coat, the grand hat. She looked beautiful, but very old-fashioned. And yet at the same time, she looked right. Not uncomfortable, as Bel would in those clothes. Charlotte looked as though she wore that sort of thing every day.

"I'm dreaming," Bel whispered to herself. "It's still early morning. I dreamed that I woke up, but actually I haven't at all. In a minute, Gran'll come and tell me to get up, and that she's bought me chocolatey cereal as a special treat."

"What did you say?" Charlotte leaned in closer. "Isabella's ever such a pretty name, I like it. And Bel. My little sister calls me Lottie sometimes."

"Oh, is your sister out here, too?" Bel asked, looking around. Now that she had decided this was a dream, she felt a lot less worried. She was probably dreaming it because of the booklet Gran had given her to read. That was why Charlotte looked so familiar, Bel realized, smiling to herself.

She was the girl from the photograph, with the white cat!

Bel nodded thoughtfully. She'd seen all those photos of the house as it used to be, and now her mind was just bringing them back. Not that she actually remembered seeing a Christmas tree in any of the pictures. But she was sure she'd seen something like it in a film, maybe, or on TV. At the end of the dream Bel was sure she would crawl back under the tree, and come out with the house looking as it always did, and then she'd wake up. For now, she might as well just enjoy having somebody to play with in the snow.

Charlotte's face had paled at her question, Bel noticed now. She looked at Charlotte worriedly. Bel hadn't meant to upset the other girl, but the cold-reddened skin on her face looked odd now, the pinkness had gone into strange patches on the tops of her cheekbones and the tip of her nose. "No," Charlotte murmured. "Lucy's still in the house. She's in bed, actually. She isn't well." She hung her head, and Bel saw her shoulders heaving, as though she was trying not to cry.

"Oh, I'm sorry." Bel cast around for something to say. "My gran says there's a horrible cold going around. I'm sure your sister will be better soon." She knew that this was all a dream, but she had to say something nice – Charlotte was so upset.

Charlotte glanced up at her, and managed to smile, but she didn't look very comforted. "Maybe. It was just a cough, to start with, but then Mama said the doctor called it influenza. She's been in bed for so long. Days and days. And Mama said that Lucy had a fever, when I asked her yesterday." She crouched down to stroke the white cat, and perhaps to hide her face, Bel thought. "Then I woke up in the middle of the night and Mama and Miss Laney, that's our governess, they were on the landing outside my bedroom door. They were talking in whispers, but I got out of bed and I could almost hear them. They said Lucy's temperature was dangerously high, and she might go into convulsions." She glanced up at Bel. "Do you know what that is?"

Bel shook her head. "No..." she whispered.

"I don't, either. I wanted to ask Mama about it this morning, but when I went to see her, she'd been crying. I could see by her eyes. And then somehow I couldn't ask her. The words just stuck in my throat." Charlotte pressed her fine leather gloves against her throat, as if it hurt. "I think Lucy is a lot worse than Mama or Miss Laney will tell me."

"I'm sorry..." Bel whispered. She didn't know what else to say. Influenza was the same thing as the flu, she knew that. Mum had said that if you actually had proper flu, not just a cold, it was nasty. But it wasn't dangerous! Charlotte was talking as though her sister *was* really seriously ill. Then Bel frowned as she remembered her class trip to the museum. There had been a Victorian pharmacy shop on display, and Mrs Abbott had told them that medicine was very different back then. There weren't nearly as many medicines, and the ones they had weren't as useful. People still used all sorts of strange remedies, like mustard plasters and leeches. People could die from something as silly as a cut finger, if it got infected, and mothers often died giving birth to babies.

Bel shuddered a little, even though this was all a dream. It was making her think about Gran, and the way her horrible winter cough wouldn't go. "My gran isn't very well, either," she murmured. "I worry about her, too."

Charlotte jumped up and took her hand, and squeezed it. "Oh! I can feel how cold your hand is, even with my gloves on! You shouldn't be out here without gloves and a proper coat!" Then she looked worriedly at Bel. "But maybe you can't afford a coat…" she murmured – she was obviously trying to be tactful about it.

Bel opened her mouth to explain that she did have one, but she'd just been in too much of a hurry to put it on. But then she stopped. Even inside a dream, it might be difficult to explain to Charlotte that she was a hundred and fifty years in the past. Maybe it was better to let her keep on thinking that she was a poor child from the village.

"Shall we run about?" Bel suggested. "I'd get warmer then." She laughed as the white cat wove around her ankles eagerly, purring. "Would you like to run?" she asked. "I didn't think you liked the snow on your paws."

Charlotte smiled. "He does love chasing after Lucy and me though. He's really Lucy's cat. An old lady in the village gave him to her as a kitten, because Lucy admired him so. He's called Snow." She rolled her eyes a little. "Lucy was only six – she couldn't think of a more interesting name. I wanted to call him Maurice."

"He's beautiful," Bel said, crouching down to stroke Snow under the chin. She could feel him purring, the thick white fur trembling under her fingers. "And so big! I don't think I've ever seen a bigger cat."

"I wish he wasn't so big," Charlotte sighed, looking worriedly over towards the woods. "He thinks that he's even bigger than he actually is, and he fights with the dogs from the village. He usually wins, but look at his ears."

Bel peered at them, and sucked in her breath. "Oh, you have been fighting," she said to Snow. "All those bits missing!"

Snow gazed back at her so smugly that Bel couldn't help laughing. His expression said that she ought to see what the dogs looked like.

"He's so determined that all the garden and the grounds belong to him," Charlotte explained. "But the children from the village play in the wood on the edge of the grounds, and sometimes their dogs slip through the fence. I have to keep watching out for Snow, now that Lucy's not well."

She shivered. "There's one dog – a big black one called Jack. You've probably seen him, I mean, he's *very* big. Snow's fought with him before, and I had to run and fetch a bucket of water from the water butt in the kitchen gardens and throw it at them. Snow was so cross with me. He scratched me and Lucy as we took him away, and Jack growled and kept showing his teeth at us. The boy he belonged to said he was sorry, and he'd make sure he never let Jack come in the garden again, but I've seen the dog in the wood, sniffing around the gaps in the fence. The boy said he wasn't really fierce, and he can't help chasing cats, but I'm not sure I believe him." She sighed, and picked Snow up, tickling his ears. "We got into such trouble, because we were so wet. Miss Laney says that's why Lucy's cough got worse, and it's my fault for not looking after her better."

"That's nonsense!" Bel shook her head firmly. "How could it be the cold water?" She was sure influenza was a virus, it wasn't to do with being cold at all.

"You don't think so?" Charlotte said gratefully.

"No." Bel smiled at her. "I should think your governess was just worried and cross. Sometimes my mum tells me off for something that isn't really my fault, and then says sorry afterwards."

Charlotte sniffed. "Miss Laney wouldn't do that, even if she knew she'd made a mistake. She got one of my sums wrong once when she was explaining how to do it, and she swore I hadn't heard her right." Then Charlotte sighed. "But she's staying up all night to nurse Lucy, so I shouldn't say bad things about her, whether or not I— Oh!" She turned to look back at the house, and gently pushed Bel more into the shadow of the trees. "That's her. She's calling me for breakfast. Don't let her see you."

Bel could just hear someone calling in the distance, and she wriggled further between the branches.

Charlotte ducked her head, embarrassed. "You're very nice, and I have liked talking to you, but I don't think you're supposed to be here. I don't want you to get into trouble."

Bel smiled at her. "That's all right. I'd better go, too." Surely she was going to wake up soon?

"Will you come back?" Charlotte asked eagerly. "Please? You're much more interesting to talk to than those stuffy Marshall girls at the Vicarage. Or Lady De Vere's niece. She can't even walk a step without calling her maid to pick something up, or change her shoes, or bring her a parasol. It's very boring."

"I'll try..." Bel said, a little doubtfully. Could she? Perhaps if she read the history booklet again at bedtime, and put it under

her pillow, she'd dream of Charlotte again.
"I promise. I'll try my best. Goodbye!"
She waved to Charlotte as she hurried
back to the big fir tree, and ducked
underneath the spreading branches. She
could see Charlotte waving back, with
Snow dangling under her other arm. The
big white cat looked most undignified,
and he was wriggling.

This time Bel was paying more attention to the path under the tree, instead of hurrying after Snow. When she felt that strange pulling sensation again, the odd feeling that she'd thought was her cardigan catching on a branch, she knew what it was. She was home – back in her own time. She stumbled up from under the branches and round the twist in the path, and looked curiously at the house. Glass doors again, and the sign that said Oak House Sheltered Accomodation.

Bel sighed. The house looked a lot less interesting now. It had been such a strange, real sort of dream. She was quite sad that it was almost over.

CHAPTER FIVE

"Gran, have you ever had a dream that felt real?" Bel asked, as she stirred the chocolate-brown milk in her bowl.

"Oh, yes." Gran looked at her thoughtfully. "For a long time after your Grandpa died, I had dreams where I was absolutely certain he was still alive. It was wonderful to see him, because I was missing him so much, even though it made me sad when I woke up."

Bel nodded. "But you did know the difference? You didn't go on thinking that the dreams were real?"

Gran stared out of the window for a moment before she looked back at Bel. "Yes… Yes, I suppose so. A couple of times I did realize that I was remembering something that had happened in a dream, and thinking it was real."

"Mmm." Bel watched the swirls in the milk again, and sighed. "Sorry, Gran. I didn't mean to make you sad."

"You couldn't, darling."

Bel smiled at her, but then the smile faded. She hadn't woken up.

She was pretty sure she hadn't, anyway. When she'd walked back across the lawn, Gran had been waving to her from the windows, delighted about the beautiful snow, but just as worried about Bel catching cold as Charlotte had been. She had promised not to go out without her gloves and big coat again.

Now it felt like the day was just carrying on and on. And apart from the bit where she'd travelled back a hundred and fifty years and played with a Victorian girl, it was so normal.

But if it hadn't been a dream, then what was it?

All day long, Bel kept looking out of the window towards the shrubbery, wondering if it would happen again. When she went out to build a snowman, she couldn't help sneaking glances behind her at the dark trees. Did she want to go back? She'd love to see Charlotte again, of course. But if she ever did, it would only be because something truly strange had happened. Something magical. And that was scary. Very scary. Bel had been fine when she thought it was all just a dream, but she wasn't so sure now. What if it went wrong? What if she got stuck in the past and couldn't ever get back? Or she did something that changed the future in some awful way? So many bad things could happen.

But at the same time... It was so exciting! Could she really give up on this chance? The choices tore at her all day, and she went to bed still unsure.

The next morning, though, Bel woke up and crept out to look at the snow again, just as she had done the day before. There was a little ball of worry in her stomach. What if all the snow had gone? What if that strange winter magic had melted away, too?

But as soon as she came into the living room, Bel could tell from the odd whiteness of the light that the snow still covered the garden. The joy and relief that surged through her told her the answer. She had to go back and find Charlotte again.

This time, Bel thought more carefully about what she would wear. Charlotte still thought that she was a girl from her own time, so she needed to dress as though she was. She couldn't wear jeans, or any sort of trousers. Luckily, she had a pretty dress that Gran had given her, with a long, full skirt. Bel had complained about it to Mum when Gran first bought it, and Mum had promised that she'd only have to wear it when Gran came over. It wasn't that Bel really hated the dress, it was just so frilly. But it was exactly right for Charlotte's time. She'd wear her knitted cardigan over the top again, but with thick gloves and a hat this time, too. Her hat was just a knitted bobble hat, nothing like Charlotte's amazing feathered one, but Bel wasn't pretending to be the rich daughter of a factory owner, she was just a girl from the village. It would be fine.

Gran was still asleep, so Bel wrote a note and left it on the little table by the window. *Gone to play in the snow. Back soon!* She giggled as she wrote it. Back soon – or back in a hundred and fifty years. She wasn't quite sure which.

Her footsteps crunched as she headed across the lawn. There had been a big freeze overnight, and there was a thin crust of ice over the snow. Bel shivered as she reached the shelter of the trees, and hurried round the icy path to the fir tree. Then she caught her breath as she stared down at the dark branches. What if it didn't work? What if she couldn't make the journey back in time by herself?

Suddenly sick of worrying and thinking, Bel flung herself down beneath the branches. She had to try, whatever came of it. She squirmed over the pine needles, peering towards the snowy path on the other side. Then the strange dragging feeling caught at her, and she laughed. It *was* happening again, and it definitely wasn't a dream!

She crawled out on to the path, looking around eagerly for Charlotte or Snow, but she couldn't see them at first. Then she heard a voice calling, beyond the shrubbery. "Snow! Sno-oww!"

Bel peeped round a tall holly bush and saw Charlotte in her red coat. "Hello!"

"Oh! You came back!" Charlotte hurried towards her, looking worried.

"I'm so glad. Bel, you haven't seen Snow, have you? I can't find him. Lucy asked me to take special care of him, and now he's disappeared."

Bel shook her head. "No, I haven't. But I've only just arrived. Shall I help you look for him? Oh, but can I? What if someone from the house sees us, won't you get into trouble?"

"I don't care," Charlotte said stubbornly. "It's much more important to find Snow. And besides, I can't believe there's anything wrong with playing with you. You're perfectly nice. If Mama complains I shall tell her that you were in the woods and you heard me calling and offered to help look for him. She won't mind." Charlotte nibbled her bottom lip, and glanced sideways at Bel's clothes, as though there was something that worried her. Perhaps it was her boots, Bel thought. Charlotte had said they looked odd before.

But then Charlotte shook her head, as though she'd decided it just didn't matter. "I don't think Lucy's getting better," she said, all in a rush. "Mama's been crying again, her eyes had red rims all round them, and her voice is hoarse. If we can find Snow for Lucy, she won't mind who I play with."

Bel followed her out on to the lawn. "Where's the best place to look?"

Charlotte sighed. "Probably along the edge of the little wood. That's where he likes to go, to climb the trees and tease the dogs from the village. Maybe we can help each other over the fence."

Bel nodded, gritting her teeth. She didn't much like the idea of a wood full of fierce dogs, but she was desperate to help Charlotte and Lucy. She couldn't help wondering what would happen if she got bitten by a dog in the past. Would it actually hurt? Would the bite still be there when she went home? She scurried after Charlotte, trying to put the thought out of her mind.

They jogged all along the fence line, calling for Snow, but there was no answering mew, or scurry of white through the snowy bracken.

"Oh, why does he have to go and get lost now?" Charlotte wailed. "Lucy will want him when she wakes up, she's certain to ask for him."

"Charlotte! Charlotte!"

"That's Mama!" Charlotte whirled round. "Oh, Bel, I have to go. I'll see you soon, I hope. I'm coming, Mama!"

Bel ducked behind a clump of ivy that was growing out over the fence, and watched Charlotte dash towards her mother.

"Oh, there you are, darling! Will you come and sit with Lucy for a few minutes?"

Mrs Armstrong did look dreadful, Bel thought. Her face was so pale that her tired eyes looked practically scarlet, and she was clutching a bedraggled shawl around her shoulders – she'd obviously just thrown it on to come and look for her daughter.

"Is she any better?" Charlotte asked.

Her mother sighed. "No, darling, I'm afraid not. Do you know where Snow is?

She was crying for him, too."

Charlotte shook her head, glancing back
guiltily towards the fence and the wood.

"Never mind. She'll be glad to see you. Charlotte…"

"What is it?" Bel caught her breath at the frightened look on Charlotte's face.

"Try not to let Lucy see that you're worried, darling, please. She doesn't realize how ill she is." Charlotte's mother hugged her. "She's still so feverish that I don't think she would notice, anyway, but try not to cry in front of her, won't you?" She led Charlotte away, her arms still wrapped tightly around her, as though she was afraid to let her go.

Bel shivered. She wanted to go back home to Gran, or even better, to Mum and Dad and her own cosy bedroom, where she didn't have to think about such sad, frightening things. But Snow was out here somewhere. What if it really would help Charlotte's sister to find him? She straightened up slowly, edging out from behind the clump of ivy, and then gasped. They were there, in front of her. How could she have missed them? In a neat little procession across the snow were small, faint pawprints. Cat-sized pawprints. They disappeared under the ivy, where it had grown over and around the fence, and weakened the wooden slats. There was actually quite a big hole. Perhaps this was where the dog had slipped through before?

Bel took a deep breath, and crouched down to wriggle through the hole. She did it before she'd properly thought about it, because she knew if she took the time to think she would run straight back to the shrubbery.

The wood was dark after the brightness of the snowy lawn, and Bel came up blinking. It was quiet among the trees, and eerie. When she first tried to call for Snow, her voice came out in a whisper. Swallowing, she tried again. "Snow! Snow!" But there was only the sound of a bird, squawking and fluttering in a tree high above her.

Bel set her teeth and trudged through the bracken, which was brownish and soggy and loaded with snow. She kept calling, but she heard nothing, until there was a deep growl behind her.

Gasping, she whirled around, staggering and slipping in her boots. Standing between her and the fence was the dog that Charlotte had described – a huge black dog, snarling at her.

"Go away!" Bel quavered, but the dog came towards her instead, still growling, the sides of his mouth drawn up to show red gums and yellowish teeth. He was nothing like any dog Bel had met before. She quite liked dogs, or at least she didn't not like them. But this one was a monster.

Bel was sure that the dog was going to leap at her, but he didn't. Instead it stopped a couple of metres away, sinking into a crouch, his front legs flat on the ground. He stood there, growling a low, steady warning, and Bel stared back at him like a trapped rabbit. But then, after a minute or so, her mind began to work again. Perhaps the dog had been trained not to hurt people?

Very, very slowly, she began to edge around him, keeping the same distance apart, but working her way back towards the fence, and the hole. The dog turned with her, watching her all the time, his eyes angry. When she was in line with the fence again, Bel walked slowly backwards away from the dog, clenching her fists tightly inside her gloves, wondering if he would follow her. But he only watched, the growls lower now and fainter, like breaths. At last she came up against the fence, gasping as she banged into it. It seemed to have taken hours just to cross those few metres of ground. She crouched down, as slowly as she could, and wriggled back through the hole. Then once she was out on the lawn again, she turned, and ran.

CHAPTER SIX

Bel spent the day letting Gran teach her how to knit, but it didn't work very well. She'd wanted something to distract her from the dog, and the thought of Charlotte and her little sister. She felt guilty, as though she'd abandoned them. She had tried to find Snow, but the dog had been just too scary. She'd hoped that knitting would stop her thinking too much, but Charlotte's frightened face, and her mother's red eyes, kept slipping back into her head. If only she could have helped them find Snow for Lucy. What if the little girl was still crying for him, and making herself worse? By the time Gran suggested stopping for hot chocolate and biscuits, Bel had only managed a couple of rows, and they had holes in.

She lay awake for what felt like a long

time that night, wishing she had been brave enough to go back. She could have told Gran she wanted some fresh air, or just some more time to play in the snow. Then she could have tried to help Charlotte. Or at least told her about the pawprints.

When Bel fell asleep at last, she dreamed strange dreams, full of flickering images. White cats raced past her in the dark between the trees, and a dog growled low. Bel woke up panting in fright, clutching at the duvet. She sat up in bed, trying to slow down her panicked breathing, and telling herself that it was only a dream. But even though she'd only been dreaming, Snow was probably still lost, and Lucy was still sick and crying for him. Bel wanted to help so much, but the real dog had been even more frightening than the growling dream creature, and it was the middle of the night now. Bel didn't think she was brave enough to go out to the shrubbery in all that blackness.

She couldn't lie down and go back to sleep though, not while she was thinking about Charlotte and Snow and Lucy. She got out of bed and pulled on her dressing gown, creeping through the flat to the big glass doors. She could see the shrubbery… Bel found she was pressing her fingers against her mouth, her heart thumping. "If Charlotte knew about the pawprints," she whispered to herself, "she'd go and search the wood for Snow, even if the dog was there. I know she would. She was so worried about her sister, she'd do anything. But she doesn't know." She shivered. "So I have to do it for her.

And for Snow, and Lucy."

Biting her bottom lip, Bel pulled on her coat and a scarf, then thick socks under her boots. She remembered the little torch that Gran kept in the kitchen drawer, and fetched it. She couldn't go into that wood at night with no light, however wrong it was to have an electric torch in 1860. It wasn't as if *she* was supposed to be there, either, so the torch couldn't be that much of a problem. She let herself out of the glass doors, glancing reluctantly back at the warm flat behind her. Then she hurried down the terrace steps before she could change her mind, marching out across the snowy grass towards the wood.

A few snowflakes floated lazily down, and she shivered, and walked faster, eager to get to the shelter of the shrubbery.

She crawled under the fir tree, a tiny part of her hoping that the magic would have gone, that she wouldn't be able to go back. But then she gasped, feeling that strange pull as she broke through time.

She was there – she could do this, she had to. Bel stood in the safety of the pretty, trimmed trees, gazing at the wood, wild and dark in her faint torchlight. She gripped the little torch tighter, and made for the hole in

the fence, swallowing back her squeaky, frightened breaths.

Bel tramped deeper between the trees, listening hopefully for a mew, or the padding of cat paws. And then beneath the fluttering beat of her heart, she heard it again – not Snow, but the low, snarling growl of a dog, and then a flurry of loud barks. She felt her heart thump even faster, and her stomach twisted with fright. Bel wanted to turn and run. But she was sure that the dog had something to do with Snow's disappearance – that barking definitely sounded like he was excited about something…

Bel crossed her fingers, wishing and wishing that the black creature hadn't hurt Snow. She covered the torch with her hand, dimming the light so the dog didn't notice her coming closer. The growls and whines sounded louder now, as though he must be only metres away. Bel tiptoed through the trees, peering cautiously through the darkness, and there he was.

The black dog was standing at the bottom of a huge oak tree, growling and clawing at the massive trunk.

The dog still hadn't noticed her. He was sniffing and huffing and growling around the base of the tree. As though he wanted to climb up it.

Bel took a couple of steps closer, and then peered up into the tree, through the great lacy network of branches, trimmed in snow. "That's why he's so excited," she whispered to herself. "I thought that clump of white was just more snow." Then she giggled, excited and silly with the relief. A pair of gold-green eyes was shining down at her in the light of the torch. "It *is* Snow... It's him, it's Snow! I've found him!"

But now she had to get him down. Bel swallowed hard, and took a step forward. "Here, Jack!" she called.

The dog turned sharply, his ears laid back. He lowered his head suspiciously, and paced forward, growling deeply at Bel. She felt the hair on the backs of her arms rise up, and it took everything she had not to turn and run. "H-here..." she called again, patting at her knees. The dog came closer, so close that even in the dim light of the torch, Bel could see his eyes glittering. "Good dog!" she muttered, and coughed, trying to make her panicked voice come out as more than a croak. "Come on. Come here." She walked back a few steps, patting her knees again. "That's it... You follow me..." She looked sideways, trying to see if Snow had realized what she was doing.

Yes! He was further out along his branch now, looking down at her. His fluffy white tail was swishing to and fro, as though he was confused, not quite sure what to do.

But as Bel watched, he leaped down to a lower branch.

A tiny smile twitched the corner of Bel's mouth. It was working!

Then the dog sniffed at the air suspiciously, and Bel's eyes widened. "Here, boy, here, Jack!" she called frantically. "Come here! Snow, watch out!"

Snow darted back along the branch with an angry hiss, and the dog growled uncertainly, clearly not sure who to chase first, the girl or the cat. Then he turned, diving for the tree.

"Don't you dare!" Bel shrieked, dashing after the great black dog as he sprang for the tree. "Come back here! Leave him alone!" She was shouting so loudly that the dog reared back in surprise, letting Bel get between him and the tree.

"GO AWAY!" Bel screamed. "Go home!" She flattened herself against the tree trunk, grateful for the solid bulk of it at her back, and flashed the torch in the dog's eyes, so that he muttered and whined. "Get back!"

But the torchlight didn't hold him for long. The dog came closer, breathing one low, constant growl, and Bel knew he wasn't going to let her go.

She was trapped.

CHAPTER
SEVEN

"Are you all right?" Bel whispered to Snow, flinching a little as the dog turned to eye her suspiciously. He was refusing to leave the bottom of the tree now. He obviously thought that Bel and Snow would try to escape if he moved away.

The white cat stared down at her from his branch, his gold-green eyes glowing in the torchlight. Bel thought he looked grateful that she was there. "I haven't been much use," she whispered. "Sorry... But he'll let us go soon, I'm sure he will, and then we'll run."

Bel stood watching the dog pace back and forth in front of her, letting out deep, breathy snarls. Surely he'd have to give up eventually? Or wouldn't his owner come looking for him? Perhaps the boy wouldn't notice he was gone until the morning though. Bel sighed – that was too late. Lucy needed Snow back now. Wearily, she leaned back against the oak tree, and saw the dog prick up his ears again. He was watching for any movement. "It's all right," she murmured. "I'm just trying to get comfortable. Since you won't let me go."

The oak tree was enormous – it was strange to think how many hundreds of years it had been growing in these grounds. There were great fat roots coiling through the ferns around her, and Bel danced the torch over them, wondering if there was somewhere she could sit. She was so cold she could hardly feel her toes, and she was starting to feel sleepy, too.

Then she smiled – there was a hole

among the roots that looked almost like a little cave. She snuggled into it, pulling her knitted jacket around her tightly. At least she had thick socks and her boots on. She wriggled her toes and fingers, trying to keep them as warm as she could, and fought against her yawns. She mustn't go to sleep. As soon as the dog got bored and went home, she had to take Snow back to the house. She mustn't fall asleep. She mustn't...

Bel twitched and sighed, and snuggled down further. Her duvet must have slipped off, she was so cold. And her bed was not at all comfortable. Maybe she'd fallen asleep while she was reading, and she was lying on her book? Everything was so lumpy. At least her toes were warm.

Bel opened her eyes, blinking wearily, and then sat up with a jump. Her torch was glowing faintly in her lap, enough to see that it was still dark. She was huddled up in the tree roots, but something was different. *How* were her feet warm? She leaned forward a little, peering at her boots in the dim glow of the torch and then caught her breath in a tiny squeak. The black dog was lying on her feet.

As she stared, he slowly lifted his head and gazed back at her with dark, sleepy eyes. Then he opened his mouth in a huge yawn, so that the torchlight glinted on his yellowish teeth. He slumped back down across her feet with a sigh.

Bel swallowed. Maybe his owner had been right, and he wasn't quite so fierce after all... He just hated cats. But she was still scared of him, even if he was a very good foot-warmer. "Good dog," she whispered faintly, and he made a strange sort of grumbling noise in his throat. It didn't *sound* fierce. More just sleepy. Bel leaned forward, holding her breath. The boy had told Charlotte that Jack wouldn't bite. She reached out and patted his ear, very gently. It was surprisingly soft and silky for such a big, fierce-looking creature. Jack made the grumbly noise again, and sighed, and then Bel felt a warm wet tongue lick across her wrist. He liked her!

Bel opened her eyes, and stroked him again, rubbing both ears, and then running her hand over the top of his head, and down his back. Jack twitched and wriggled, and his tail slapped against the snow with pleasure. Bel chuckled. "Did you want a nice stroke, then?" she murmured, leaning forward and starting to rub his head and ears with her other hand as well. "I wish we'd known you were friendly to start with. But you didn't look at all friendly, you know. And as soon as you see Snow again, I think you might turn into a terror." Then she glanced down, wondering what the strange crinkling noise was. The dog had noticed it, too. His ears had pricked up, and he was looking hopefully at Bel's coat pocket. "What have I got in there?" Bel muttered. "Oh! Sweets! That bag of toffees Gran gave me." She reached into her pocket, gasping as she banged her numb fingers on the tree roots. "Ow…

It's so cold. I hope Snow's all right, up in the tree. I didn't even think to look, I was all taken up with you." She pulled out the paper bag of toffees, and tried to peer up at the oak tree. But the fading torchlight didn't stretch that far – the tree was only a deeper shadow in the darkness. Jack nudged hopefully at her hands, making the bag of toffees rustle again. She could hear his tail swishing against the snow, too.

"Do they smell good?" Bel murmured. "Do you like toffee? I suppose they do have toffee in your time, don't they? It's an old-fashioned sort of sweet."

Then she frowned at the dog. "If you're hungry, and you really want my toffees, maybe you'll do as you're told." Slowly, painfully, she stood up, muttering "Ow," every time she straightened out a cold-cramped bit of her. "I'm even more grateful that you slept on my feet," she told the dog. "I think if you hadn't I'd just have fallen over when I tried to stand up."

He was standing up too now, still sniffing eagerly at the bag of toffees. Bel smiled. "Come on, then." She picked up the torch, and hooked it on one of her fingers, so she had both hands for unwrapping the sweets. "There you go." She held out the toffee to the dog, and then panicked for a second as he pounced on it, remembering those yellowish teeth. But all she felt was a soft, damp snuffling as he gobbled it out of her hand. "Good dog…" She walked a few steps across the clearing, in the direction she thought Charlotte had pointed when she talked about the village. Then she glanced back, looking anxiously up into the tree. She could see a faint white shape, shifting a little in the darkness. Snow was watching. "Have another, come on…" Jack bounced along beside her eagerly, occasionally barging her a little bit when he thought she was being too slow with the toffees.

At last the trees began to thin out, and Bel was sure she could almost see the looming shapes of houses. They were coming to the village. "What am I going to do if you just follow me straight back again?" Bel murmured, feeding Jack another toffee. "Just because you're being nice now, it doesn't mean a thing, does it? One whiff of cat and you'll be a fierce beast again." She peered into the toffee bag. It looked like there were about three left, plus all the wrappers for him to sniff at. Was that enough to distract him for a few minutes? Would it give her enough time to run back through the wood and rescue Snow?

Bel frowned. It was all she had. She opened the bag, and held it out for Jack to sniff. He tried to shove his huge muzzle into it, his tail wagging madly, but she pulled it away, and flung the bag further down the path. "Go on! Go find it!" she called. She paused for just long enough to watch him dash after the bag, before she turned and ran.

The torch waved madly as she raced back through the wood, sending shadows whirling across her path. But Bel hardly saw them – she was too intent on getting back to the oak tree, and Snow.

As she dashed into the little clearing, the torch caught on a wisp of whiteness – Snow, leaping down through the branches. She hurried up to the tree, gasping for breath, and smiled delightedly as the big white cat jumped down among the ferns and brushed around her ankles, purring so loudly that Bel could feel it all through her. Then he set off through the wood determinedly, looking back to check that she was following him.

Bel glanced over her shoulder as they came to the hole in the fence, but there was no sign of Jack. Perhaps he was still trying to get those last toffees out of the bag. Then she smiled to herself. More likely he'd just eaten the bag whole.

She really hoped it wouldn't do anything awful to his insides. But then her uncle's dog ate tissues all the time, and it never seemed to do him any harm.

She ran out on to the lawn, and stopped, peering up at the house. There was a window lit, quite high up. Someone was awake.

"Bel!" There was a delighted cry from close to the house, and a figure in a white nightgown dashed across the grass to hug her. "Bel, you found him! Where was he?"

"Stuck up a tree – a big dog chased him up there. It must have been Jack, the one he fought with before. What are you doing out here, Charlotte? Did you hear us?"

"No, I woke up and I couldn't get back to sleep, I was so worried about Lucy. So I thought I would come out and look for Snow again."

"How is she?" Bel whispered.

"No one's telling me." Charlotte pointed up at the lit window. "But that's the night nursery, where Lucy is. Someone's still up there with her, even though it's the middle of the night." She gulped. "That isn't good."

Snow wove himself around their feet, mewing. It almost sounded as though he was telling Charlotte to hurry up.

She nodded determinedly, and caught Bel's hand, pulling her towards the house. "Come on."

"But I can't!" Bel looked at her in surprise. "Not if your mama is there."

"I don't care who's in Lucy's room," Bel said firmly. "You're coming, too. I'd never have got Snow back without you, Bel, and I shall tell them so. Even if you are …

I don't know what."

"W-what do you mean?" Bel stammered.

"You don't come from the village," Charlotte said, pulling Bel round the side of the house to a small door, and easing it open. "Your clothes are strange, and you say such odd things. I wonder if you're some sort of ghost." She pressed her hand over her mouth, stifling a scared sort of laugh. "Which would be very helpful, because then Mama won't see you anyway."

Bel smiled at her. "I don't think I'm a ghost. Not quite…"

"I don't care. I'm not letting you go, not now. Lucy…" Charlotte swallowed. "Lucy might be dying, and if you're a ghost, or a fairy, or some sort of magic, she needs you…"

CHAPTER EIGHT

The side door led into a sort of passage – not one that Bel had seen in her own time, it was very plain, with a stone floor and greyish paint. She guessed that it was usually somewhere that the servants went, and perhaps the children of the house.

"Oh, it's so warm in here," Bel sighed, rubbing her hands over her arms.

"I don't think it's really that warm. It's just not as cold as outside." Charlotte sat down by the door and started to unbutton her boots, hissing as her icy fingers fumbled over the tiny buttons. Bel stood on the backs of her heels, and hauled off her wellies. Snow rubbed himself around the girls' ankles, and then darted off along the passageway, stopping to look back at them impatiently.

As soon as she'd followed Snow and Charlotte up a wooden flight of stairs, and out on to a landing, Bel started to see the differences in the house at once. A lamp flickered gently in a glass globe. She was pretty sure that wasn't an electric light. And the walls were so dark – a reddish-brown colour, nothing like the pale yellows and greens in Gran's version of Oak House.

"Come on," Charlotte whispered, pointing along the landing. "The night nursery is there – do you see there's a light on?" Snow was already trotting along the landing, eager to find Lucy. The door was shut, with just a thin gleam of light leaking out from underneath. Bel smiled as the big white cat stood up on his hind legs, pawing at the wooden panels.

"Shh…" Charlotte hurried after him, and slowly turned the door handle. Snow bounded eagerly into the room, and the two girls followed him, Bel looking around curiously. There was a fire burning low in the grate, and another oil lamp, only just glowing, so that the whole room was softly lit. It smelled faintly of smoke, but Bel was sure there was an odd scent of illness, too. Perhaps it was the medicines, or some strong disinfectant that had been used to clean the room, but it was definitely there."

"That's Mama," Charlotte whispered, nodding at the woman asleep in an armchair by the side of the little bed. "She's been sitting up most nights with Lucy – she's so tired. I expect she sent Miss Laney to rest."

Charlotte's mother did look exhausted, Bel thought. She was wearing a very beautiful dress, in some sort of silk, with a shine to it, but it was creased, and she had an unfashionable apron tied over the top of it. Her hair was coming down from its piled-up style, and there were dark rings under her eyes.

But she only glanced at Charlotte's mother for a second or two. Snow had raced across the room, and leaped up on to the bed. Now he was stamping up and down over the blankets, purring and purring. The tiny lump in the middle of the bed stirred, and someone muttered, "Snow?" in a thick, muddled sort of voice. Then the child in the bed sat up, struggling to prop herself on her elbows, as though she couldn't even manage to lift her own weight properly. Charlotte hurried to help her, piling up pillows behind the little girl's back. "There," she murmured, looking anxiously at her sister.

"You found him!" Lucy whispered. "Where was he?" Bel flinched at the sight of her face. It was so thin, and there were burning red patches across the tops of her cheeks. Even her hair looked thin and flattened and ill.

"Trapped up the big oak tree, with that dog from the village barking at him," Charlotte said impressively. "Bel had to entice the dog away with toffees – she was a heroine."

Lucy leaned a little further forward. "Who are you?" she asked faintly, peering at Bel.

Bel opened her mouth, but she didn't

know what to say. She wasn't sure Lucy would remember whatever she said, but Charlotte would...

"She's someone who came to help," Charlotte told her sister. "She rescued Snow for you."

"Oh..." Lucy nodded vaguely. "That's good." Snow had finally decided on the absolute best part of Lucy's bed to snuggle in, under her arm, with his head tucked up right on her shoulder, and he was still purring like a little engine. The purr seemed to be

making Lucy sleepy – she leaned back against the pillows, her head drooping, a faint smile on her face.

"She's asleep again," Bel whispered worriedly. "Did we wear her out?"

"I think so." Charlotte flattened the pillows a little, and tucked the blankets up around Lucy's shoulders. Then she knelt down beside Lucy's bed to watch her closely. "But look at her – she's not as flushed, is she? It was the fever that Mama was most worried about. Lucy was so hot, it was making her see strange things." She smiled at Bel. "She'll probably think that you were just a fever-dream. But I'm sure she doesn't look as hot now."

Bel stared at Lucy critically. Maybe Charlotte was right – the scarlet blotches across her cheeks did seem to be fading.

"Even if it doesn't work," Charlotte said, her voice wobbling. "She's happy. She's not worrying about Snow any more. That's what I wanted."

Bel swallowed hard, and crossed her fingers behind her back. Lucy couldn't die, surely. She was so little...

Charlotte got up from beside the bed, and stumbled, almost falling over. Bel caught her arm. "Are you all right?"

"Sleepy," Charlotte murmured. "And cold. Aren't you? We should sit by the fire."

"Yes…" Bel sighed. "I should go home, before your mama wakes up. But I'll just get warm first. The fire's so nice." They crouched on the hearthrug, holding out their hands to the flames, almost purring themselves as the heat softened the ache in their cold limbs.

Charlotte leaned against her mother's chair, sighing and stretching out her toes to the fire, and Bel watched her, smiling. In a minute she'd go, when her fingers had thawed out properly. She rubbed her hands together, resting her head on Charlotte's shoulder, just for a moment...

Bel woke up with a start, panicking. How could she have been so careless? Charlotte's mother would be awake any minute, and how was she going to explain what she was doing in the night nursery? What if the family called the police? Did they have police back then, Bel worried vaguely, pulling at her duvet. It was only as she sat up that she realized she wasn't still curled up on the rug by the fire.

She was back in her own bed, as if it had all been a dream.

"It wasn't," she whispered, looking around her little room. "It couldn't have been. I knew things – I saw things I didn't know about, I mean. Like the lamps, and Charlotte's clothes. Charlotte and Lucy and Snow, I can't just have made them up, can I? It was real. Oh, please say it was real!"

Bel climbed out of bed, and realized that she still had her coat on. She smiled. She'd never have worn her coat to bed, would she? It was only a little thing, but still... She walked out into Gran's living room, where her wellingtons were neatly lined up beside the glass doors. Bel wasn't sure what she was looking for, but there must be something. Some sort of proof that she hadn't dreamed it all.

She stood in the middle of the room, turning slowly, but there was nothing. It looked just the same as it always had. A pretty, rather boring room, with Gran's ornaments dotted around, and the tiny Christmas tree glittering with tinsel in the corner. Bel felt her eyes begin to sting with tears. They *had* all been real, Charlotte and Lucy and Snow … hadn't they?

She slumped down in Gran's armchair, tugging the knitted blanket Gran had made around her shoulders for comfort. There were some papers tangled up in the folds of the blanket, and she pulled them out wearily, throwing them on to the little table. It was the booklet with the history of the house, she noticed, without really thinking about it.

Then she sighed. Of course. It was just like Mum had told her – dreams were pieced together from bits of things that had really happened. She had read it all in the booklet – she'd even seen Charlotte's picture, and Snow's. She must have made the rest of it up from things she'd learned at school, odd bits from films. She'd probably seen oil lamps somewhere.

Bel picked up the booklet, and flicked through it to find the picture of Charlotte and Snow. "Maybe in my dream I made up the story about Lucy being sick to explain why you looked so serious," she whispered, as she turned the pages.

Then she stopped, gazing down at the brownish photograph. At the two girls, and the plump white cat.

It wasn't the same.

It was Charlotte *and* Lucy. Snow was in Lucy's arms, and though they all looked quite solemn, Bel was sure that was only because the photograph had taken ages, like Gran had told her. Snow was a little blurred, as though he'd been wriggling. She traced her finger over them lovingly, smiling at Lucy's plump cheeks – so different – and Charlotte's proud big-sister look, the way she had her hand on Lucy's shoulder. She wondered how long after Lucy's illness it had been taken.

"It worked. I brought him back for you," Bel murmured happily.

She bounced out of the chair, wanting to go and tell Gran. Then she stopped, frowning down at the booklet. Would Gran believe her? She wouldn't say it was all a dream, Bel was almost sure. She wouldn't want to hurt Bel's feelings. But she'd have that little smile, the one that meant she was going along with it, but she didn't really believe.

Bel closed the booklet carefully, stroking it flat. It wouldn't matter if she kept it, there were lots of them on the reception desk downstairs. The picture would be her secret.

"I wonder if I'll ever see you again?" she murmured, turning to look out of the glass doors at the shrubbery, and the fir tree. Would it work, if she crawled underneath the tree again? Or had it only taken her back in time because Charlotte and Lucy needed her? Bel touched her fingers against the cold glass, torn. Part of her wanted to dash outside and try, but something held her back. Perhaps it was better not to know. Then she could always think that maybe, one day…

Something moved in the purplish early morning light, and Bel's heart jumped. The snow had shifted, as if something white had walked across it. Something like a white cat. Had Snow come back again? It had been Snow she'd seen first, after all. She pressed closer to the glass, peering eagerly at the snow-covered terrace, and then she gasped.

Not Snow. Instead, a tiny white cat was staring up at her. As she watched, he stood up against the door, pressing tiny shell-pink pads against the glass, and opening his even pinker mouth in a mew. A snow-white kitten, just as demanding as the cat she'd known so long ago. A kitten of her very own – after all, Mum and Dad had said that she could have a cat. "Where did you come from?" she whispered. "Did Snow send you to me?"

The kitten scrabbled at the glass, and mewed again, and Bel laughed, reaching for the door handle, to let her own little snow cat in.

Bel danced the ribbon up and down, and the white kitten stood up on his back legs, batting at it so madly that he nearly fell over backwards.

"Are you going to open any more presents?" her gran said, laughing. "Usually you can't wait to tear into them, Bel!"

"I know." Bel laid the ribbon down on a pile of wrapping paper, and watched Snowball fling himself at the rustling mass. He wriggled and bounced and squeaked as the paper crunched underneath him. "He's just so funny, Gran. He keeps distracting me from my presents."

"He is lovely," her mum said, wafting a little piece of wrapping paper in front of Snowball's nose. "I do wish we knew where he'd come from though. I can't help thinking that someone must be missing him, but no one's called and we did put posters up… I just can't imagine giving him back now."

Bel smiled down at the present Dad had just handed her. She knew exactly where Snowball had come from – Snow and Charlotte had sent him to her. She didn't know how, but that didn't matter. Snowball was her very own – he was their thank you.

STAINED-GLASS WINDOW BISCUITS
(makes about 12)

YOU WILL NEED:

100g unsalted butter, at room temperature

60g golden caster sugar

125g plain flour

1/2 tsp mixed spice

About 12 coloured boiled sweets

You'll also need biscuit cutters – Bel and her gran used star-shaped ones, but you can use any shape.

METHOD:

❄ Preheat the oven to 160°C/320°F/
Gas Mark 3. Line two baking trays
with baking parchment.

❄ Mix the butter and sugar with a fork
until smooth. Add the flour and mixed
spice and mix in.

❄ Lightly flour a board and, using a floured rolling
pin, roll the dough out to about 5mm thick. Cut
out your stars and put them on the baking trays.

❄ Now you need to make a space for the
stained glass. You can use a smaller cutter that's
the same shape if you have one, or you can use
a plastic milk bottle top to make a circular hole
that's just the right size. Make sure to leave about
1cm of biscuit all around the hole, otherwise your
finished biscuits will be too delicate to take off
the tray. Keep cutting out biscuits until all
the dough is used up.

✳ Put a sweet in the centre of each biscuit, and then pierce a hole (if you want to hang the biscuits as decorations) in the top of each using a straw or cocktail stick.

✳ Bake in the centre of the oven for 15–20 minutes, then take them out. Don't worry if they don't look quite done – they'll harden up once they're out of the oven.

✳ Leave the biscuits on the tray to cool for ten minutes to give the stained-glass centres time to set. Then remove from the parchment and leave to cool properly on a wire rack.

❄ Thread a ribbon through the holes
and hang them up somewhere
sunny – or just eat them!

THE WINTER WOLF

FROM BEST-SELLING AUTHOR
HOLLY WEBB

Amelia is exploring the huge, old
house where her family are spending
Christmas when she finds a diary
hidden in the attic. It was written
by a boy struggling to look after an
abandoned wolf pup. Before she
knows it, Amelia is transported into
the wintry world of the diary.

Noah wishes he had someone to
help keep a lost wolf pup safe.
Then Amelia appears mysteriously
one day. Together, can they find
the pup's mother out in the
icy wilderness?

HOLLY
WEBB

Holly Webb started out as a children's book editor, and wrote her first series for the publisher she worked for. She has been writing ever since, with over one hundred books to her name. Holly lives in Berkshire, with her husband and three young sons. Holly's pet cats are always nosying around when she is trying to type on her laptop.

For more information
about Holly Webb visit:

www.holly-webb.com